Come Here Spinner!

Written by Shirley-May Paterson
Illustrated by Martin Bailey

Once there was a very busy spider who lived at Morningside School. She lived in a classroom with the children who were five and six years old. Her name was Selina Spider and she had two children. Their names were Weaver and Spinner.

Weaver was a very busy little spider who followed Selina in and out, up and down, over and under, and round and round all day long.

Spinner was a lazy, good-for-nothing spider. Spinner was never there when it was time to repair the web. Spinner was never there when it was time to hunt, and Spinner was never there on time for meals.

On Monday, Selina Spider made a delicious shoofly pie.

She called out, "Come here Spinner, it's time for dinner."

But Spinner wasn't there! He was spinning in the art corner – all you could see was hair!

On Tuesday, Selina Spider made lovely mosquito and fly shish kebabs.

She called out, "Come here Spinner, it's time for dinner."

But Spinner was on the run, chasing rainbows from the crystals hanging in the sun.

On Wednesday, Selina Spider made deep-fried flies' feet, which Spinner especially liked.

She called out, "Come here Spinner, it's time for dinner."

But Spinner didn't show! He was crawling on a table with his feet in the play dough!

On Thursday, Selina Spider made a great big pot of beautiful fly-by soup.

She called out, "Come here Spinner, it's time for dinner."

But Spinner had gone ahead and was sleeping like a baby in the home corner bed!

On Friday, Selina Spider made a wonderful flea-fly-flan.

She called out, "Come here Spinner, it's time for dinner."

But Spinner decided to disappear and Selina never looked behind the Teddy Bear's ear!

On Saturday it was very quiet in the Morningside School and Selina cooked up a great big plate of flies and fries.

She called out, "Come here Spinner, it's time for dinner."

But Spinner was gone! He was very nearly swept up when the cleaner came along!

On Sunday, Selina Spider cooked up real roast flies.

She called out, "Come here Spinner, it's time for dinner."

But Spinner, who had spun right out, had fallen in the fish tank and was trying hard to shout.

"Helglugglugglug!" "Helglugglugglug!"

While Selina Spider gasped with fright,
Weaver made a special flight
skimming just above the water,
such a daring, darling daughter,
scooped right up that naughty Spinner
and told him it was…

Then with a safe but soggy Spinner,
the family all sat down to dinner.

He wiped the water from his eyes
and humbly ate his roasted flies!